UNCLE ARTHUR'S
BEDTIME STORIES

Book One

Arthur Maxwell

"They that be teachers shall shine
as the brightness of the firmament;
and they that turn many to righ-
teousness as the stars for ever and
ever" (Dan. 12:3, margin).

Review and Herald Publishing Association
Washington, DC 20039-0555
Hagerstown, MD 21740

Printed in U.S.A.

Contents

Amy out for a walk in the park with her doll carriage.

© S. W. P.

Amy's Gift

About Two Little Girls and a Doll

"ARABELLA," said little Amy lovingly, as she laid her baby into its red-and-black carriage and carefully tucked the covers in around it, "I am sure there is not another doll in all the wide world so lovely as you."

Arabella did not reply, but laid herself back serenely on the white pillowcase, and closed her eyes as if perfectly contented with her lot.

"I think we will go for a walk, now, Arabella," said Amy, and pulling the garden gate shut behind her, she sallied forth with her precious charge down the street.

"Arabella," said Amy sternly, "I do hope you behave yourself while we are down town. And, mind, if you cry, you won't get any sweets."

Needless to say, Arabella did not cry, and indeed behaved herself as few babies do.

Amy enjoyed the walk immensely, feeling very proud of herself, as little girls do when they go out with a doll's cart all alone.

On reaching the end of the street, Amy met a poor little girl carrying the dirtiest, raggedest doll you ever saw.

"Arabella," whispered Amy, "I'm so glad you're not as dirty as that."

But the poor little girl seemed to love her dirty, ragged doll just as much as Amy loved Arabella.

She was hugging it very tightly to herself, and telling it that it was just the loveliest doll in all the world.

At this moment, just as the poor little girl started to cross the road, a motor dashed around the corner. The little girl jumped back and saved herself, but in her fright she let go of her precious dolly, which rolled away underneath the motor and was crushed to fragments.

The poor little girl burst into tears as she witnessed the sad fate of her treasured dolly. It was the only one she had ever had.

Amy's loving little heart was touched immediately. What could she do? Nobody was about, and it seemed that it was for her to comfort the poor little girl. Running to her side, she put her hand on the little girl's shoulder and told her not to cry. But the little girl cried on.

Amy looked at her carriage and thought of her beloved Arabella. Could she? Could she?

"Poor little girl," she said, "don't cry any more. You may have my very own Arabella. She is the beautifulest doll in all the world, and she will surely make you happy again."

Giving Arabella one last hug and kiss, she handed her over to the poor little girl, who could scarcely believe her eyes.

"For me?" she said, "for me?"

"Yes," said Amy, "for keeps." And Amy turned away and ran back home as fast as she could, lest she should change her mind. Then she sat down on the front doorstep and thought of what had happened, and looked, with tears, into the empty doll carriage.

But somebody had seen what had happened. High up in one of the near-by houses a big lady had been looking out of the window, and had watched the loving deed. A few days later that same big lady called at Amy's home with a long, brown-paper parcel in her arms. She said it was a new baby for a little girl who had given her own away.

Amy was so happy she just didn't know what to do. She said Jesus must have sent this wonderful parcel, and mother said she thought so, too.

Amy called the new dolly Isabella, to remind her sometimes of the one she had loved so much before.

Mother's Present

FRANK was very much puzzled. There were two birthdays coming along soon in his home, and he just didn't know what to do about them. Like most little boys, he was very "hard up," and to buy two presents seemed impossible.

He decided to speak to mother about it, although that was difficult, as one of the birthdays was hers. Anyhow, he thought, mother always understood, and perhaps he would get an idea of what to do while they were talking.

It so happened, however, that mother herself opened up the subject.

"Frank dear," she said one afternoon, "you won't forget Uncle Herbert's birthday, will you?"

"No," said Frank, "I won't forget Uncle Herbert's, but," lowering his voice to a whisper, "there's another one besides."

Mother smiled. "But Uncle Herbert's is the more important, you know," she said.

"I don't think so," said Frank, with a note of certainty in his voice that made mother's heart beat faster with joy. "Of course, I want to please Uncle Herbert, but I want to make *you* happy!"

At this lovely gesture of devotion, mother had to stop what she was doing and put her arms around Frank and kiss him, which made Frank forget all about trying to find just what kind of birthday presents he should give.

The days passed, and soon the morning of

mother's birthday dawned, and still Frank hadn't been able to make up his mind what he should do.

He went off to school greatly perplexed. What could he do now? Oh, why hadn't he decided before!

Then it suddenly dawned upon him that he couldn't buy anything that day in any case. The stores would all be closed by the time he could get to the city. He felt angry and ashamed of himself for having left it until late, after all.

All through his classes he could think of nothing else; for how could he go home to mother and have no present for her?

Then a bright idea came to him. At least he could write mother a letter. She might be glad of that. It would be a different sort of present, anyway.

The more he thought of it, the more he liked the idea. So in the interval between classes, he found a corner where he could be alone, and there he wrote his birthday letter to mother.

He told mother how much he loved her, and that he wanted to grow up to be a good man and earn money so that he could buy her all the lovely things he would like to buy her now but couldn't, and that he would always love and care for her as long as she lived.

The letter written, Frank sealed it carefully, and on reaching home, crept up to the front door, dropped it in the letter box, made a big "rat-tat" like the postman, and then ran away to give mother time to read it.

When he returned, there were tears in mother's

eyes, but a very sweet smile on her face. She said that the letter was the loveliest present Frank could possibly have sent her.

And when, four years after, I met this mother on a train one day, and she told me the story, she said to me, "That letter is the most precious treasure I possess."

Perhaps *your* mother would like to have a birthday present like this, someday, from you. I wonder!

ELEANOR CAMPBELL

© S. W. Partridge

Leaving the sinking ship

The Stowaway

The Story of a Captain's Sacrifice

OME years ago a small steamer encountered a terrific storm in the South Atlantic Ocean. For three days the ship was tossed and buffeted by the mighty waves. One mast was carried away, and the steering gear was damaged.

Toward the close of the third day, the storm seemed to increase in severity. The sky became blacker than ever, and the poor sailors realized that still worse times were ahead. Suddenly, amid the crashing of awful peals of thunder, the cry was raised that the ship had sprung a leak.

In a moment the pumps were manned, but soon it was discovered that the water was rising in the hold faster than the men could pump it out. They worked desperately for another hour, but all in vain. Seeing the task was hopeless and the ship was doomed, the captain ordered that the boats be lowered.

To the dismay of all, it was now discovered that there was but one of the boats that remained undamaged by the waves—the rest were so battered that no one could expect them to live in such a sea. There was nothing to do but to cram the entire crew into the one boat.

Quickly the men climbed in, filling the boat to its utmost capacity. There was just room enough to squeeze in the captain, who, like the noble Englishman he was, had remained behind till the last.

He was about to step over the side of the ship to climb down the ladder to the boat, when, hearing a cry, he looked around. There, running toward him across the deck, was a strange young lad, dirty-faced and clothed in rags. He was a stowaway.

Where the lad had hidden himself or how he had kept himself alive since the ship left port, the captain did not know, and there was no time to inquire.

"Quick, lad!" he shouted, stepping back on to the ship. "Down the ladder!"

The lad needed no second invitation. He was over the side and into the boat in a moment—filling the last few inches of space.

"Come on!" shouted the men to the captain, willing to overload the boat rather than leave him behind.

"Push off!" yelled the captain, above the howling of the storm. He knew full well that one more in the boat would certainly capsize it and cause the death of all.

So the men pushed off, and not a moment too soon. Hardly were they at a safe distance from the ship than it turned on its side and plunged into the sea, bearing the noble captain to his ocean grave.

After many days of hardship, the men in the boat were picked up by a passing vessel and finally reached home again. Never did the stowaway forget the captain's self-sacrifice. The memory of that heroic deed changed his life. He felt he must be worthy of so priceless a gift. In his pocket he carried the captain's photograph, to which he would point as he told and retold the thrilling story, saying, "He gave his life for me."

And, now, children, does not this story help us to understand what Jesus has done for each one of us? He is the Captain, we the stowaways. We do not in the least deserve to be saved and have a place in His beautiful home. But Jesus died to make this possible; and although it was many, many years ago that He made His wonderful sacrifice, it is available for every one of us to-day. As the stowaway afterwards talked about the captain, so we, too, should be glad to tell others of what Jesus has done for us. We, too, can say, "He died for me."

Just-a-Minute Janet

"JANET! Janet!" called mamma

No reply.

"Coo-oo, Janet!" she called again, going to the kitchen window to see what Janet was doing.

"Just a minute, mamma," came a little voice from the garden. "I shan't be long."

"But I'm waiting for you," called mamma. "I want you to come now."

"Just a minute," came floating back from the invisible Janet.

"Dear me!" exclaimed mamma to herself. "How tired I am of hearing her say, 'Just a minute.' Just wait till she comes in!"

Five minutes passed. Then ten minutes. But no Janet appeared.

"Janet!" called mamma, going to the window again. "Come here at once!"

"Just a minute!"

"Oh!" said mamma, "if I don't—"

But at this moment Janet's little face popped around the corner of the toolshed smiling so sweetly that mamma didn't know what to say next.

"Here I am," said Janet pleasantly. "Did you call, mamma?"

"You heard me call," said mamma, trying to look stern. "Why didn't you come at once?"

"I was busy," replied Janet demurely. "You see, I was washing dolly's clothes."

"Maybe you were," said mamma, "but when your mamma calls, you must obey at once. It's very rude to keep mamma waiting ten whole minutes before you come to her."

"Yes, mamma," said Janet.

"And don't you ever say, 'Just a minute,' again."

"No, mamma."

"All right," said mamma, "now take these eggs around to Mrs. Jones."

Janet took the parcel and ran off happily, humming a little tune to herself. But while she was gone she quite forgot all that mamma had said.

When she returned, she went out into the garden again to her "washtub" behind the shed. Oh, what fun it was rubbing and scrubbing and making soapsuds just like mamma! And she had a clothesline all for herself, some of mamma's clothespins, and a real scrubbing board. No wonder she was happy!

But by and by a familiar voice was heard again.

"Janet! Janet!"

The reply was equally familiar.

"Just a minute, mamma!"

"So she has forgotten already," said mamma. "Then she will have to learn some other way."

Once more the minutes passed—five minutes, ten minutes, fifteen minutes. Still no sign of Janet.

But meanwhile mamma went on with her dinner, and when she had finished, cleared the table. She was half repenting of her decision when an unusual sound caught her ears.

"O mamma, mamma! Come quick! come quick! The water's all spilled over me!"

Suddenly a bright idea came to mamma. Feeling sure that nothing serious had happened, she called out:

"Just a minute, Janet!"

"Oh, come quick! come quick!" wailed Janet; "my shoes are full of water!"

But mamma did not stir. She merely called back once more, very deliberately,

"Just a minute, Janet."

At this the poor, soaked Janet appeared around the corner. What a picture she looked! As she had jumped off the stool after hanging dolly's frock on her line, she had brought the whole basin full of soapy water on top of herself.

Mamma couldn't help laughing. It was too funny for words.

"Why didn't you come when I called?" said Janet very crossly. "Can't you see I'm all wet and horrid?"

"I couldn't," said mamma. "You see, I was busy. I had to clear the table after dinner."

"Is it as late as that?" asked Janet, looking surprised.

"Yes," said mamma. "And I have been waiting for you all this time. If you had come when I called, this wouldn't have happened."

Janet saw the point, and a faint little smile flickered across her dear little face. And, of course, that was the end of it; for mamma ran to get her some dry clothes *and* some dinner, while Janet promised once more that she really never would keep mamma waiting again.

Held Up by a Robin

YES, it was a whole railroad system that was held up, and by a little robin redbreast, too!

Two little girls told me the story, and I am sure it must be true, for it all happened close by the town where they live. And, from what they said, everybody was talking about it for weeks.

It all began one afternoon when a freight train was slowly steaming out of the station. It had not traveled very far when the brakeman noticed that a little robin was flying alongside the train.

"Look at that bird!" he said to a man who was with him. "It's following us."

"So it is! It seems to be trying to get underneath this caboose. But I suppose it will fly off soon."

But the bird kept flying close to the caboose, and as the train gathered speed, it flew faster and faster. After a while, however, the pace became too swift for it, and the poor little bird had to give up. It flew off and perched on a tree, gradually becoming smaller and smaller as the train steamed on, until at last it was out of sight.

Why the brakeman should bother about one little robin redbreast I don't know, but perhaps it was because the bird looked so sad as it gave up the race and perched on the tree. Anyhow, as soon as the train stopped at the next station he jumped down and looked underneath the caboose. And what do you suppose he found there? Away underneath in a corner was a robin's nest, with three pale-blue eggs in it!

Now he knew why the poor little bird had been flying so fast! But where was Mrs. Redbreast now? he wondered. Could she have followed?

He held up the train as long as he dared, hoping she would catch up in time to get back to her nest, but she did not come. At last he had to give the signal to go, but before doing so he walked up to the engine and chatted with the driver, telling him all about the nest, and particularly about the eggs.

Now the driver of that freight train had just as kind a heart as the brakeman; so he promised to drive with special care, so that the eggs would not be jolted out of the nest. And how gently he brought that train to a stop every time! If he had had the President on board he couldn't have done it better.

So the train ran all the way to its destination and all the way back again. And at every stop the brakeman got out and looked underneath to make sure the eggs were there.

At last the return journey had been made, and the train was back in the home station. But where was the mother bird that had last been seen perched on the branch of a tree many miles out along the railroad line?

She was not far away. Indeed, even as the brakeman stood looking underneath once more, there was a sudden fluttering of wings, and faithful Mrs. Redbreast dived under the caboose and sat on her nest again.

But now what to do? Of course the brakeman could have forgotten all about it, but he didn't. Having taken so much care of those eggs all day long, he felt a special interest in them now. So he told the stationmaster what had happened, and he came over to see the robin.

The stationmaster said that the best thing to do would be to disconnect the caboose and shunt it onto a siding until the eggs were hatched. You see, he had a kind heart, too, as big as that of the driver and the brakeman. But the trouble was that, to do anything like this, he had to get permission from the head office of the railroad; and what excuse could he give for holding up the caboose? Furthermore, there was another difficulty. This was the only caboose available for this particular train, and how could they get another one before this train had to leave the next day? Would the head office be willing to send another caboose all the way down the line just because a robin was sitting on a nest? Not very likely, thought the stationmaster. But, being such a kind-hearted man, and anxious to help the poor little bird if he could, he decided to phone the head office and ask. They could but refuse.

Now it so happened that, by this time, the news about the robin's nest under the caboose had spread all through the town. The brakeman had talked about it and the engineer had talked about it; and then their wives and their children began to talk about it, until the whole town became excited, and people by the hundred were streaming down to the station to see this unusual sight.

As you can imagine, when so many men and women and boys and girls were all running to one place, the newspaper men became interested, too, and they ran down there with their pens and their notebooks and their cameras and what not. So, within a very short time the news of Mrs. Redbreast's adventure was on the front pages of the local papers.

News like this travels fast. In fact, it reached the head office of the railroad before the stationmaster was able to speak to the man he wanted on the telephone. By great good fortune, this proved to be another man with a heart as big and kind as that of the stationmaster, the brakeman, or the engineer. So when the stationmaster asked if he could have another caboose, so that Mrs. Robin should not be disturbed, the official replied, "Of course! That caboose is not to be moved under any condition until the eggs have been hatched."

The next day another caboose arrived just in time for the train.

Well, Mrs. Robin sat there on her nest day after day like a little queen on her throne, smiling—that is, if robins do smile—at all the hundreds of children and grownups who came to look at her. And then one great day the eggs were hatched and the proud mother began feeding her little brood. Orders then came from the head office that the caboose was not to be moved until all the baby birds had been taught to fly and had left the nest. So the little family stayed on as guests of the railroad until they decided to go somewhere else.

And now, just think of those four men upsetting the program of a railroad for the sake of one little bird! What a lot of kindhearted people there still are in this sad old world! And how much simple joy their thoughtfulness for one of God's smallest creatures brought into the lives of hundreds of their fellow men!

ARTHUR MAXWELL

What Charlie Heard in the Market Place

A True Story

CHARLIE was in the market place, playing marbles with a chum. Hearing some one speaking loudly, the two looked up and saw a crowd gathered around a man who was standing on a small platform.

"It's the minister!" said Willie.

"Let's go and hear what he's talking about," said Charlie.

They ran across the market place, and pushed their way through the crowd so as to get as near the platform as they could.

When they found that the minister was preaching a sermon, they were not a little sorry they had come so far in, and tried to get out again. But they couldn't move. All around the crowd was pressing them in.

Seeing that they could not get away, they began to listen. Charlie did not understand much of what was being said, but somehow one sentence seemed to fasten itself on his mind. It was the text upon which the man was preaching: "If thou save not thy life to-night, to-morrow thou shalt be slain." 1 Samuel 19:11.

All the way home Charlie thought about these words, and wondered what they meant. He could not get them out of his mind. They worried him.

About ten o'clock that night, Charlie's mother was sitting quietly in the kitchen knitting something for the baby, when a voice from upstairs called her.

"Mamma!"

"Go to sleep, Charlie," called mother; "you should have been asleep long ago."

Half an hour later mother thought she heard some one crying. Curious, and a little anxious, she put down her knitting, and crept upstairs. Yes, to be sure, Charlie was weeping softly.

"Charlie, whatever is the matter?" asked mother lovingly.

"I'm frightened," said Charlie, amid sobs.

"Why, what has happened?"

"Mr. Brown was preaching in the market place this evening, and he said that if I didn't save my life to-night, to-morrow might be too late, and I might be killed."

"I'm sure he didn't mean it just like that," said mother soothingly.

"Yes, he did," said Charlie, with a strange earnestness in his voice. "How can I 'save my life to-night'? What did he mean?"

"I will tell you about it to-morrow," said mother. "Go to sleep now; you must be tired."

"No, mamma; I must know now. Tell me."

So mother stayed, and began to tell him the story of salvation. She had talked to him before about Jesus, but Charlie had never seemed to listen. Mother realized that this was her opportunity.

She began by telling him how, in the long, long ago, Jesus made the heavens and the earth and placed the first parents of man in the beautiful garden of Eden—how they disobeyed Jesus, and how their children became more and more wicked as the years went by.

"But Jesus loved them still," said mother, "and He sent many messengers to tell them of His love and to ask them to come back to Him. But they would not listen to them. At last, after a long time, Jesus decided to come down from heaven Himself to make plain how real was His love for men.

"So, leaving behind all the glorious things that were His in heaven, He changed Himself into a little child, and grew up as all boys grow. When He became a man, He went about telling people of His love for them, all the time healing their sicknesses and helping them every way He could.

"He told them, too, that if only they would believe in Him He would freely forgive them for all the wicked things they had done, and save them from the punishment that would otherwise certainly come to them. He also promised to give them eternal life— to come back for them some day, raise them from their graves, and take them to live with Him forever.

"They were wonderful promises to make, especially to people who had been so unkind to Him," said mother; "and you would think that everybody would have come to Him with joy.

"But no; instead, they took Him and nailed Him to a big wooden cross, hanging Him up in the air until He died. It was an awful thing to do to Jesus, the King of heaven. I wonder sometimes why it was that God did not open the heavens and send the angels down to punish those wicked people. But He didn't; He wanted to give them still another chance.

"Jesus was buried in a tomb by a few friends, but within three days He came to life again. After that He met with those who had believed in Him, and told them that He was now going back to heaven, but would keep His promise to come again. To-day He is still in heaven; but soon He will come back in all His glory, and take those who love Him to be with Him forever."

"But how can I be sure He will take me?" asked Charlie.

"The Bible says, *'Believe* on the Lord Jesus Christ, and thou shalt be saved.' And that is really what Mr. Brown meant when he talked about 'saving your life to-night.' He really wanted you and all the people in the market place to acknowledge Jesus as Lord of heaven, Saviour of the world, and their own best Friend. If you do that, you need not worry any more about what may happen to-morrow or in years to come, for you will belong to Jesus. He will take care of you all your life; and if He thinks it best for you to die before His return, He certainly will not forget you when He does come back. He would not be happy in heaven if you were left out. Do you understand about Him? Do you believe in Him?"

"Yes," whispered Charlie, squeezing mother's hand. "I am not afraid now."

Mother went downstairs, very happy to know that her boy had given his heart to Jesus. She knew that if he faithfully served Him day by ·day, his life would be safe, and he would have nothing to fear.

"A Whole Loaf, Please"

How a Hungry Girl's Prayer Was Answered

(BASED ON AN ACTUAL HAPPENING)

IN THE days following the awful revolution in Russia there was much suffering among the people of the country. Many thousands starved to death. Thousands more, who once had had all that they could wish for, became beggars. It was difficult for the children to understand, for the change came so suddenly upon them all. I think many of them must have "cried their eyes out" lots of times.

There was one family that I know about that had a very hard time. Father had been killed, mother had died, and grandma was left with three children. Once they had lived in a beautiful home, and their table had always been spread with good things. Now they were living in a hovel. Grandma was knitting hard all day to try to earn enough to keep the children alive. But when she had done her work, it was very difficult to obtain food in exchange for it. There was so little food to be had.

One day the last morsel had been eaten. After a crust apiece for the midday meal, there was not a crumb left in the house. Grandma was very, very sad, but she tried not to let the children see her anxiety. She called them around her, told them what was the matter, and then they knelt down to pray. She felt that they had come to the end of their resources, and that unless Jesus should help them they would surely die of starvation like the other poor people around them.

So they prayed. What a prayer meeting that was! Just grandma and the three children; but they all prayed as only the starving can.

I don't know what they all said, but the little girl's prayer was like this:

"Dear Jesus, please send us something for supper; not just a crust, but a whole loaf, please."

They had not seen a whole loaf for many a long day, and it was like our asking for a birthday cake for an ordinary meal.

Supper time came, but still there was no food. Poor little dears! How they must have longed for something to eat!

"You haven't sharpened the bread knife yet," said the little girl to grandma, still fully believing that her prayer would be answered.

So grandma sharpened the knife, according to Russian custom.

The evening passed, and night drew on. Cold and hungry, the children were about to go to bed when there was a knock at the door.

A man stood outside, covered with snow. He had tramped nearly twenty miles that day. Grandma recognized him as an old friend of the family, and welcomed him in.

"What has brought you here to-night?" she inquired.

"About noon to-day something impressed me that you were in dire need and that I must come to you at once."

Then, turning to the children, he said: "And you will never guess what I have brought with me."

"I can," said the little girl.

"What is it, then?" asked the gentleman.

"It's a whole big loaf," said the little girl.

"And that's just what it is!" said the friend, opening his overcoat and drawing one out. "And how did you know?"

Then they told him how they had prayed that Jesus would send them not a crust, but a whole loaf, and together they went down on their knees and thanked Him for His wonderful care for those who believe in Him.

And though it was only a loaf and no butter on it, what a wonderful supper it was they had that night!

The Picnic

It was wash day, and mamma was so busy that she didn't have a minute to spare for little Doris.

"Oh, dear! What shall I do, mamma? I haven't anything to do at all," said Doris.

"You mustn't bother me so," said mamma. "Run along, dearie, and look at one of your picture books. There, the boiler's running over again. Doris, you mustn't keep on coming into the wash house. The steam will give you a cold."

Poor Doris went out and shut the door, feeling very sorry for herself. She didn't want to look at her picture books, for she had seen the pictures so often she was tired of them.

It was a beautiful, warm morning, with the sun shining brightly. Doris decided to go into the garden. Through the garden fence she saw little Kathleen, who lived next door. She seemed to be as lonely as Doris herself, and for the same reason. Her mamma was washing too.

They had had a quarrel the day before, and said they wouldn't speak to each other again. But Doris thought that maybe for this once she would forgive Kathleen and make up. After all, anything would be better than being lonely.

Preparing the Lunch

"Kathleen!"

"What do you want?"

"Let's be friends," said Doris.

"Why?"

"Because I want some one to play with. Shall we have a game?"

"What sort of game?" asked Kathleen, getting interested, and coming over to the fence.

"What would you like to play?" asked Doris.

"Oh, something different."

"Well, what can we do?"

"I know what I'd like to do," said Kathleen.

"What?"

"I'd like to go for a picnic; it's such a lovely day."

"Oh, yes!" said Doris. "So would I. But our mammas wouldn't let us; I'm sure they wouldn't."

"Let's ask them," said Kathleen.

" They're both too busy washing," said Doris, " we shall get punished if we do."

" But let's try," urged Kathleen.

To the little girls' surprise both mammas were quite agreeable to their going for a picnic together, provided, of course, that they did not go too far and that they got everything ready themselves. Strict instructions were given as to the place they were to go, where they could easily be found if necessary.

Now all was happiness. Kathleen's mamma said she wouldn't mind if they prepared the food in her house, so in they both went. Kathleen cut the sandwiches, and Doris wrapped them in waxed paper and put them in the picnic basket, which was the prettiest little basket you could wish to see.

Good-by!

Lunch Time

Then they found the little tent that Kathleen's daddy had bought for them to use in the garden, and rolled up an old piece of blanket so that they would not sit on the damp ground. Of course they decided to take a kettle with them, because this was going to be a really-truly picnic.

Then they started off. The two mammas found time to come away from their washing to wave good-by to the two little girls from the front gate. They were glad to have the children happy.

The girls had not gone far, however, before they made the discovery that while they had brought the tent, the blanket, and the kettle, they had left the lunch behind! In the excitement of saying good-by, they had actually forgotten all about the most important thing. So back they had to go to get it.

Now they were off again, and very happy little girls they were. They did not go very far away, but to them it seemed miles and miles. They made up all sorts of stories as they went along, and imagined they were really grown-up big people going for a real picnic.

Presently they came to the quiet little place on the beach to which they both always loved to come. They had been here many times with their mammas, but this time it was all quite different. They both felt so important.

Somehow they managed to get their tent put up. It was quite a big job for such little people, but they felt they must do it all properly.

The tent fixed, they both thought it must be time to have something to eat. So they opened the all-important lunch basket, and began to take out all the little packages they had put in it so carefully just an hour or so before.

How nice everything tasted! so much better than a dinner at home! Really they had never had such a lovely meal before. If their mothers could have seen them eating the plain bread and butter as if it were sugar cookies, they would have been surprised. Perhaps they would have decided to have that for dinner every day!

How quickly the lunch basket was emptied! There didn't seem to be half enough in it. Doris and Kathleen were so hungry that they ate up everything they had brought; there wasn't even a crumb left.

Then they played games and told stories to each other. Soon the afternoon passed and the time came to pack up. Down came the tent, the blanket was folded up, and the empty lunch basket slung over Doris' shoulder. Then they started for home.

"Haven't we had a lovely time?" said Kathleen.

"Haven't we!" said Doris. "And only yesterday we said we wouldn't speak to each other any more."

"I'm glad we made up," said Kathleen.

"So am I," said Doris.

Just then they turned the corner of the road, and there, right in front of them, were two mammas standing at the gate of Kathleen's house.

"We're so glad you've come back safely," they said. "We were just coming to look for you."

Then there were hugs and kisses, a nice supper, a bedtime story, and a trip upstairs to dreamland.

Going Home

37

The Mysterious Letters

"WELL!" exclaimed Miss Simpkins in the teachers' room one morning. "I never saw such an unruly bunch of youngsters as those Hendersons. They invited me round to tea last night and I did have a time of it. As for their manners at table they were simply awful."

"Poor Mrs. Henderson!" said Miss Dawson. "She certainly has a problem with three like Gladys."

"I should say so," said Miss Simpkins. "And you should have seen them grabbing for their food, each one taking the best of everything, and, my dear, actually eating with their knives!"

"I suppose the poor woman has too much to do," said Miss Dawson.

"Perhaps she has," said Miss Simpkins, "but I think she should try a bit harder to reform their manners. It will be so difficult for them when they grow up."

If only the teachers had known, Mrs. Henderson was trying her very best to reform the manners of her three lively children. She had noticed all their bad behaviour during Miss Simpkins' visit and was deeply distressed about it.

"Whatever will teacher think of you all?" she had said almost before the door had closed upon Miss Simpkins' retreating figure. "I'm thoroughly ashamed of you, yes, all of you! Surely when your teacher is here, Gladys, you could have set a better example. It was simply terrible. And you can take it from me that we shall not have anyone else to tea for a very long time."

"Oh Mamma," said Doris, "I did so want Miss Dawson to come next week."

"Oh dear, no!" exclaimed Mamma. "Not after this. Until you children have learned to behave better in company there is no one coming to tea in this house."

"But if Gladys has Miss Simpkins, surely I can have—" began Doris.

"Not until you have all ceased to be little cannibals," said Mamma.

The subject was dropped, but it did not leave Mamma's mind. What could she do to make her children behave better when strangers came in? They were quite normal at ordinary times, but just as surely as someone came on a visit they became excited, and lost their heads. They seemed to know that Mamma would not reprove them in front of a stranger, and made the most of it.

For several days Mamma thought it over, for she knew she must find some way out of the problem. She could not have the family let down like this. At last one morning she struck a bright idea. All day she worked it over in her mind and when the children came home from school she had it ready for them.

They thought it was a great scheme and agreed to start practising it immediately. Doris was especially enthusiastic as Mamma promised that if they would all fall in with the plan she would agree to Miss Dawson being invited to tea next Wednesday evening.

They all had lots of fun over Mamma's idea during the next few days, and as it seemed to be working beyond her best expectations she gladly agreed to the invitation for Wednesday being sent.

"Now you're in for it," said Miss Simpkins when Miss Dawson showed her the invitation she had received. "I hope you come out of it alive."

"Well, it will at least break the monotony of life," laughed Miss Dawson. "I shall certainly be interested to see what happens."

Wednesday evening arrived. At the appointed time Miss Dawson was welcomed to the Henderson home and sat down at the tea-table. There she found three demure little girls sitting as still as mice.

"Strange!" she thought. "This isn't what I expected to find. Miss Simpkins must have been mistaken."

The meal proceeded. They all talked about the weather, school, games, and other things, and gradually the children became more lively. Doris reached forward with a jammy knife towards the butter.

"How many marks did you get for arithmetic today?" asked Mother. Then, under her breath, "B.K."

"Six," said Doris, blushing just a little, while the jammy knife went back on her plate.

At this moment Mamma caught sight of Beryl, the youngest, about to pour her cocoa into her saucer.

"Oh, Beryl," she said, "would you like to show Miss Dawson that scarf you have knitted for your dolly after tea?" Then, under her breath again, "N.D."

"Yes, Mamma," said Beryl, putting the cup back

in its place and stirring the contents vigorously. "Shall I get it now?"

"No, not yet. Afterwards will do," said Mamma. Then, very quietly again, "M.I.C."

Gladys, who had been eyeing the last piece of bread and butter rather anxiously, now reached forward and took it.

Then the cakes were passed round.

"I hope the weather is fine for the holidays," said Mamma, as the dish went from hand to hand. "Ahem, F.H.B."

At this Beryl, who was in the act of taking a second cake, put it back as carefully as possible, while Doris tittered.

Presently the meal was over and the time came for Miss Dawson to go. She said good-bye to the children in the dining-room and Mamma went with her to the door.

"Really, Mrs. Henderson," said Miss Dawson, "your children are good. I don't think I have ever seen a family so well behaved."

"I'm so glad," said Mrs. Henderson, beaming with pride. "It's nice to get a little appreciation sometimes."

When the teachers met in the morning Miss Dawson went straight over to see Miss Simpkins.

"So you've got back alive," said Miss Simpkins, laughing.

"Yes," replied Miss Dawson. "And I think you must have made a mistake about the Hendersons. I found them all behaving like little angels."

"You don't say so! Whatever can have happened to them?" replied Miss Simpkins.

"I don't know," said Miss Dawson. "I think their mother must have worked some magic spell over them since you were there. Anyhow, they said they were going to invite you again soon."

"Oh, rather," smiled Miss Simpkins.

But they did, and a week or two later she found herself back at the Hendersons again, watching to see whether the report given by Miss Dawson was really true. She was indeed surprised at what she found. There was a startling difference, and she tried her hardest to account for it. Once or twice she heard Mrs. Henderson whisper some mysterious letters which seemed to have a remarkable effect on the usually lively youngsters. She determined to find out what it all meant.

"I must congratulate you," she said to Mrs. Henderson as she was leaving the house. "The children have been so good, haven't they?"

"I'm so glad to hear you say so," said Mamma. "I'm afraid they weren't all they should have been the last time you came."

"Well, perhaps, er—" began Miss Simpkins. "Oh, by the way, Miss Dawson and I would love to know the secret of the magic spell you have cast over them."

"Magic spell?" queried Mamma, smiling.

"Yes, those strange letters, you know."

"Oh, did you hear them?" asked Mamma, surprised, and blushing a little. "Oh, they're very simple. You see, 'B.K.' means 'Use the butter knife,' and 'N.D.' means 'Not done.'"

"Ha! Ha!" laughed Miss Simpkins. "But do tell me what 'F.H.B.' stands for, and 'M.I.C.'"

"Well, that's really a secret. But I'll tell you. 'F.H.B.' means 'Family hold back,' and 'M.I.C.' means 'More in the cupboard.'"

"Well done!" cried Miss Simpkins. "I never would have guessed. What a splendid idea!" And still laughing heartily she said good-bye and walked down to the front gate.

Most polite!

Coals of Fire

"DADDY," cried Donovan, running in from school, "that boy Lionel is the meanest fellow in the school."

"Hello, hello, what's the matter now?" said daddy.

"Oh, he's just terribly mean. He's always calling me names, and everything I do he says is bad or stupid, and he's always setting the other boys against me with his tales."

"Tut, tut, tut!" said daddy. "It surely can't be as bad as that."

"Yes, it is," said Donovan. "And what's more, I'm not going to stand it any longer. Big as he is, I'm going to fight him tomorrow."

"Well, that's interesting," said daddy, smiling. "I hope you will tell me when it's going to come off, so I can come along and pick up the pieces."

"There won't be any pieces left of him," said Donovan vehemently.

"What? are you going to swallow him afterward?"

Donovan laughed.

"Do you know," said daddy, "I can tell you how to pay that boy back."

"Can you?" cried Donovan, all eagerness. "How?"

"Would you like to put some coals of fire on his head?"

"Anything," said Donovan. "Anything."

" Well, I'll get the prescription for you so you can do it."

So daddy went into his study and brought out a book. After a little searching he found the place.

" Ah, here it is," he said. " Listen, Donovan: ' If thine enemy hunger, feed him; if he thirst, give him drink: for in so doing thou shalt heap coals of fire on his head.' " Rom. 12:20.

" Aw," said Donovan, " that's no good; I'd rather fight him."

" But," said daddy, " this is much better. If you fight him, you cannot hurt him much; but this way you pour coals of fire on his head. You will burn him all up."

" Splendid! " said Donovan. " But I don't like that way of doing it."

" Why not try it? " said daddy. " It's worth trying, anyway."

" I'll see," said Donovan. " I'll think it over."

Donovan thought it over, and it was not long before something began to happen.

Next morning, on his way to school, who should he meet but the hated Lionel.

" Just my luck," Lionel said, as he came up with Donovan. " Got up late and missed my breakfast. Suppose you've been eating the fat of the land."

" No breakfast! " said Donovan kindly. "Poor chap! You must be hungry. Do have my lunch right now. Yes, I did have a good breakfast, so you really must have my lunch."

Lionel was as surprised as if he had received a

blow between the eyes. He looked first at Donovan and then at the lunch.

"You don't mean it," he said.

"Really I do," said Donovan. "Do take it, there's a good chap."

"Awfully good of you. Thanks," said Lionel, taking the little parcel and beginning to eat. "But you will have a bit yourself, won't you?"

Donovan took a sandwich, and they walked on to school together, munching in silence.

"Hot this morning," said Lionel, after they had gone some distance. "Wish I could get a drink somewhere."

"A drink?" said Donovan. "Let me see, where can we get one? I should like one too."

"Pity we can't get some lemonade in that store over there," said Lionel.

"I've an idea," said Donovan. "I have two dimes with me. What about it? Let's go over, shall we?"

"Well, I don't want to take your money," said Lionel. "I'll wait till we get to the playground."

"Oh, no, come along with me," said Donovan. "We'll have a glass each. Looks good, doesn't it?"

So they went in, bought a glass of lemonade each, and then hurried on to school.

That evening daddy was waiting at the gate for Donovan.

"Well," he said, "how did the fight go? I hope you won."

"I did," said Donovan with a twinkle in his eye. "I just burned him all up."

" Whatever do you mean? " asked daddy.

" Why, I did what you said. I fed him with my lunch, and I gave him a drink of lemonade, and — well, he suddenly changed. He's been as different as could be all day. We've been like old friends all the time.

" Splendid! Well done, Donovan! " said daddy. " I hope you'll win all your battles just like that."

Tell-Tale Topsy

TOPSY had one big fault. She was forever telling tales about her sister and brothers.

Just as surely as mamma went out of the house for a little while, Topsy was there on the doorstep ready for her when she came back with some story or other about the misdeeds of John or Mary or Baby Joe.

Mamma went out in the back yard on washing day to hang out the clothes. When she got back, sure enough, there was Topsy waiting with a tale.

"Mamma," she began, "Mary's been quarreling with John while you've been out."

Whereupon Mary rushed up, crying, "No, I haven't, mamma. We never quarreled; Topsy's telling fibs again."

Another time mamma went out shopping. When she returned, Topsy was there as usual to tell how Baby Joe had been tugging at the curtains and had pulled one down, how John had been talking crossly to Mary, and how Mary had dropped a saucer and broken it.

Mamma was getting tired of it. "Topsy!" she said one day, "if you don't stop telling tales about others, I shall really have to do something to you."

"But you told me to tell you if they hurt themselves."

"Of course," said mamma. "Always tell me about anything that might do them harm, but that doesn't mean you are to come rushing to me about every little fault. If Mary breaks a saucer, it is for Mary to tell me, and nobody else. Now mind, in future if the wrong person tells me about anything, or if any one brings me a tale about some petty, trivial thing, I shall fine that one a penny out of his savings box."

That was a terrible threat for mamma to make, for pennies were scarce, and there were very few in the children's savings boxes.

Of course, Topsy soon forgot what mamma had said, and the very next morning she came running upstairs, crying, "Mamma, mamma, John's spilled the milk on the tablecloth."

" A penny, please," said mamma.

" A penny? " said Topsy. " What for? "

" Telling tales," said mamma.

Poor Topsy felt very bad about it, but she had to get her savings box, take out a precious penny, and hand it to mamma. Even so she did not remember long. That same day she came to mamma with the news that Mary had torn a hole in her apron.

" Penny, please," said mamma.

" What for this time? " asked Topsy.

" Telling tales again," said mamma.

Topsy found her box again, and brought out yet another penny. But, do you know, within ten minutes she came running to mamma again.

" Mamma, mamma, Baby Joe has drawn pictures all over Mary's copy book."

" Penny, please," said mamma.

"Oh, dear!" cried Topsy, "have I got to keep on giving away my pennies? I soon shan't have any left."

"You can stop just as soon as you like," said mamma. "Just don't tell me any more tales."

Well, Topsy didn't stop all at once, but when she had paid over to mamma the very last penny in her box, with many tears she decided that she wouldn't tell tales any more.

When Everybody Helped

I WISH," said dad at breakfasttime, "I could get that wood sawed up. It has been lying about for weeks since we cut the tree down, and it makes the yard a dreadful sight."

"Aw," snorted Bert. "I don't want to saw any wood today. I'm too busy. Besides, I promised to go and play tennis with the Jones boys."

"And I can't saw anything today," said Bill. "You see, I hurt my arm the other day and—"

"But it was your left arm," interposed dad.

"I know," said Bill, "but it doesn't like for my right arm to saw anyway."

"And I just hate sawing wood," sighed Harry. "I'm too tired anyway. I'm going to play trains today. Sawing wood is the worst job I ever knew."

"And if nobody else is going to saw wood," said Jerry, the youngest, "neither am I. I'm going to be busy, too."

"That's just too bad," said dad. "I had rather hoped to have that wood out of the way today, especially as the holidays will soon be over. But there, have a good time and enjoy yourselves. Mother and I had been planning to go to the seaside this afternoon with you all if the wood had been finished, but I suppose we can go some day later on."

"Do you think he meant it?" whispered Bert to Bill when they were in the garden after breakfast.

"I suppose he did," said Bill. "Why?"

"It would be rather nice to go to the seaside," said

Bert. "I can play tennis any day. How about your left arm?"

"Seems to be getting a bit better since breakfast," said Bill.

"That's funny," said Harry. "Somehow I don't feel quite so tired as I thought I did. What would you say to—er—perhaps—er—cutting up a little of it?"

"I was wondering about that myself," said Bert.

"Let's have a look at the job," said Bill. "Maybe it's not so bad as we thought."

"And I'll help too, if you want me to," piped up Jerry.

So they went over to the fallen tree and looked it over.

"You know," said Bert, "if we really set about it, we would have the whole job done in two hours."

"Shall we try it?" asked Bill.

"Let's," they all said together, running off to the tool shed.

A few moments later they were back again with the crosscut saw, the ripsaw, the compass saw, and, in fact, every saw they could lay their hands on. Then they divided up the job according to the saws they had found and the size of the branches, and were soon busy as bees.

Dad, chancing to look out of the bathroom window, got the shock of his life.

"Mother," he called downstairs, "better start packing that lunch. They'll be done in an hour at this rate."

And they were.

Four Chocolate Eggs

WHAT excitement there was in the classroom that morning! What eagerness and attention!

You see, teacher had just announced that she was going to make a little gift to the boy or girl who answered the most questions correctly in the tests they were going to have that day.

What it was, she wouldn't say, except that it was very nice, very pretty, and very tasty.

Of course that last word set everybody's mouth watering.

"Something tasty!" said Ted Jones. "I could use that right now."

"And so could I," said Eric Foster, whose mother had been so busy that morning looking after his two little brothers and his baby sister that she had forgotten to put up his lunch.

"But I would rather have something pretty," said Peggy Phillips.

"I wonder where she put it," said Peter Rich. "Perhaps we could take a peep at it when she's not looking."

Teacher heard that.

"Oh, no, you can't," she said. "It is put away safely in my desk, and no one will see it until the tests are all over."

Peter blushed and wished he hadn't spoken.

Then the tests began, and how every one did work! When teacher asked the questions aloud, hands flashed up all over the room and waved about like trees in a high wind. When the answers had to be written, there was an unusual silence, broken only by the frantic scratching of pens on paper.

It was lots of fun, and every one had high hopes of winning the prize.

Slowly the hours dragged by, with Ted and Peter and Peggy and all the rest becoming more and more certain that they were going to win, and poor Eric getting hungrier and hungrier every minute and imagining what he would do with the prize if he should win.

At last the tests were all over, the answers all checked, and the marks all totaled up.

Who had won?

"Now," said teacher, "I am almost ready to tell you who has won the prize."

The silence was so deep that you could have heard a pin drop.

"It's going to be me," whispered Peter to Peggy.

Teacher heard again. What good ears some teachers do have!

"I'm afraid you are wrong, Peter," she said. "The prize goes to—"

"Peggy," "Ted," "Tommy," "Dick," "Amy," "Dora," came a chorus from all over the room.

"No," said teacher, smiling, "you're all wrong. Little Eric is the winner, beating Peggy by just one mark." Peggy groaned.

At this moment teacher opened her desk and produced a big chocolate egg, tied with a piece of wide blue ribbon.

"How lovely!" cried everybody. "Lucky boy," said Ted.

"Now just a moment," said teacher. "I have a second prize. It is in this box."

Every one looked and saw four little chocolate eggs.

They were good, too, but not so attractive as the big one in the blue ribbon.

Eric, blushing, came forward to receive his prize. He had looked at both prizes and was thinking hard.

Teacher smiled at him and told him how pleased she was that he had done so well. Then she proceeded to hand him the big chocolate egg. But Eric's hands were behind his back and he was blushing red still.

"Please," he stammered, "would—would you mind if I had the second prize instead?"

Everybody gasped, and teacher was so surprised that she hardly knew what to say. She had thought there wasn't a child in the room who would not have been thrilled to take the beautiful gift she was offering. But, she thought, Eric was always a good boy and he must have a reason for his unusual request. So she gave him the second prize, and Peggy was surely delighted to get the first prize after all.

Of course every boy and girl in the class wanted to know why Eric had done such a strange thing, but he wouldn't say a word. He just ran off home with his precious little box under his arm, not even opening it to take one little bite.

But if any of Eric's school friends could have peeped inside his home that evening, they would have found out all about it. For there, sitting on the kitchen floor, were four of the happiest little children you could imagine. Just three boys and one baby girl.

And they were all, in an ecstasy of delight, munching chocolate eggs.

Always Tell Mother

THIS is a school story. It's about a little girl called Gracie who used to go to a school near where I live. I don't suppose you know her, but that doesn't matter.

Gracie had a lovely home with a dear daddy, a precious mamma, and two little brothers.

Gracie loved her daddy and her little brothers very much, but I think she loved her mamma best of all. She was mamma's right-hand helper, and tried to do all she could for her. As soon as she came home from school, she would say, "What can I do to help you, mamma?" And then, as they worked together, perhaps washing the dishes or dusting or ironing,— for Gracie could iron handkerchiefs like a grown-up,— she would tell mamma all that had happened that day at school.

There was nothing that Gracie would hold back from mamma. She would tell her everything, even if she had to confess that she had had to stand in the corner for talking too much! It had become a habit with her to tell mamma all that went on, and mamma was very happy to listen, for it reminded her of the days when she went to school; also it gave her many a chance to tell Gracie things that would help her to get on more quickly.

One day a new girl came to the school, Bettie by name. She was a saucy little miss, and almost at once began to make trouble for the teacher. Some of the girls liked her because of her independent

ways, and soon it became clear that Bettie had become the leader of all the mischief lovers in the school. She was up to all sorts of tricks, some of them not very nice ones, either, and some of the stories she told the other girls were anything but good for little girls to hear.

Gracie, quite naturally, was drawn toward the bright and vigorous newcomer. She liked fun, just as all little girls do, but she was not so quick as some to make friends. There was something, too, about Bettie that Gracie did not like. She could not say just what it was, but the feeling of distrust was there just the same.

" O girls," said Bettie one afternoon just after school, " do come over to this corner of the playground; I've got such a story to tell you all. You will laugh."

The children were just out of school, and all were eager for some fun, and so together they ran over to Bettie's favorite corner of the playground.

" Now, girls, listen," said Bettie, " before I tell you this story I want you to promise me something."

" What is it? " they asked.

" Well, it wouldn't do for you to tell this story at home, you know; and you *must* promise me that you won't tell your mothers."

" All right," said some of the girls.

" Do you all promise? " asked Bettie, looking around with a superior air.

" No! " spoke up Gracie, " I shall not promise any such thing."

" Because why, pray? " asked Bettie haughtily.

"Because I love my dear mamma, and I tell her everything," said Gracie fearlessly, but turning a little pale.

"Oh, mamma's darling!" scoffed Bettie. "If you're such a baby as that, I think you had better go home now, don't you, girls?"

"Yes," said the others.

Poor Gracie blushed and tears came into her eyes, but she stood firm for what she knew to be right, and without another word, turned around and walked off the playground. She heard the other girls laughing, and guessed they were laughing at her, but she kept right on, and did not stop until she reached home.

Mother guessed at once that something had gone wrong, and she asked Gracie all about it. Gracie told mamma just what had happened, and when she had finished, mamma took her in her arms and gave her a great big hug, and said she had never felt so pleased with her little girl in all her life.

But the best thing happened in the morning. The postman brought a little note from one of the teachers. It ran like this:

"I happened to see and hear all that went on at the playground yesterday afternoon. I am sure Gracie has told you her side of it, but I felt I must write and say how proud of her I feel because she was not afraid to tell of her love for you before all the other girls. She acted like a little heroine."

And mamma and Gracie were so happy they danced around the breakfast table and nearly upset the milk.

The Flooded River

THE other day when I was telling some of the wonder-ful stories of answered prayer that I have been gathering through the years, an elderly woman asked me if she could tell me one.

"Of course," I said. And this is what she told me:

It happened in the early pioneering days when the western part of North America was being opened up, and when people still traveled in covered wagons.

A gospel camp meeting was going to be held in the State of Washington—on the Pacific Coast—and Christian people from scattered farms and villages over a very wide area planned to attend. Some faced a journey of several hundred miles over the roughest and dustiest dirt tracks imaginable in order to be present.

Such a meeting, by the way, meant giving up many weeks of time for the journey, and if any accident happened, such as a wheel coming off the wagon, or a horse or two getting lame, then the meeting might be over before the travelers could get there.

One family set off in good time for this particular meeting, but owing to various delays, by the time they reached the Snake River they had little more than a day left before the meeting was to begin.

And they found the river in flood!

Could anything have been more exasperating? Only a day left, and their path blocked by a sullen, surging stream of dangerous water!

They appealed to the ferryman and offered him an extra sum of money if he would take them over.

"Not for a million dollars," said he.

"But we shall be late for the meeting," they said, "and we have come so far to attend it."

"Better miss the meeting than drown," was the only reply they received.

But they did not want to miss the meeting, for they felt that God wanted them to be there.

So they went to their wagon, and there, on their knees, told God all about it. Of course it seemed foolish to ask Him to make the flooded river go down, but they thought of the experience of the children of Israel at the Red Sea and the Jordan, and believed God could do the same again if He so desired.

Then they looked out on the swollen stream and saw it was still in flood, rushing by with such volume and vehemence that it seemed to say, "And I shall be in flood for weeks and weeks to come."

Yet if their prayer was to be answered the river must not last like this two days, let alone two weeks. Something must happen quickly, or the meeting would be over and they would have to retrace their steps in defeat and disappointment.

They prayed again, and went to sleep that night in faith, believing that the dear Lord Jesus would do something wonderful for them.

And He did. Just what the natural cause may have been they never found out; it sufficed that the thing for which they asked came to pass.

When they awoke on the morrow, the water had dropped several feet; all danger had passed; and the astonished boatman ferried them over without question.

When the Old Ford Stopped

HERE is an amazing story that came to me recently—a story so remarkable that I'm sure you will think I have made it up. But I haven't. It really, truly happened to a minister friend of mine, and he has assured me that there's no doubt about it at all.

Some years ago this Mr. Brown—we'll call him that for now—was very hard up. He had no money in his pocket and none in the bank, and no friends to give him any.

Bills were piling up all around him, and he didn't know what to do.

His chief worry was the doctor's bill. You see, Mrs. Brown had been ill a long time, and the baby, too; and the doctor's bill had just got higher and higher till it seemed as though he would never be able to pay it.

Now they needed to go to the doctor again—but how could they when they hadn't paid the last bill? All together things looked pretty black.

So they told Jesus about it and asked Him in some way to keep His promise and supply all their need.

Then Mrs. Brown's health grew worse, and they decided that money or no money, they would have to see the doctor anyway; but how they did wish that, somehow or other, they could pay that bill they owed him first!

One afternoon they set out for town. Now their car was so old, and it rattled and shook so much as it went along, that they often wondered whether it would fall to pieces someday and drop them all out on the roadway.

They had proceeded a few miles along the bumpy country road that led to town, when suddenly the car stopped, and like some obstinate mule, refused to go any farther.

Mr. Brown looked at the gasoline, the oil, and everything else he could think of, but all in vain. Then he remembered the old saying that if a Ford stops, you should get out and look underneath to see what has dropped out by the way.

He looked, and his gaze lit upon something right underneath the engine that almost made his eyes start out of his head. It wasn't a part of the car by any means, but a curious, dirty roll of paper that looked for all the world like paper money.

Surely it couldn't be!

Forgetting everything else in his excitement, he crawled underneath the car and picked up the mysterious parcel.

Yes, it was money, real money! And the outside notes were so dirty and worn that the package must have been lying there covered with the dust for a long, long time, so that there was no hope of finding the owner.

"Look!" he cried, almost too happy to speak. "God has answered our prayer. He has sent the money we needed so much. Now we can pay the doctor today!"

And then another remarkable thing happened. Without touching the engine, Mr. Brown got back into the car and tried once more to start up in the usual way. Without a murmur the car shot forward as if nothing had ever been the matter with it.

"You know," he said to me, "I shall always believe that the angels knew that money was there and stopped the car right over it."

What wonderful ways God does have of answering His children's prayers!

The Hollow Pie

or
A Greedy Boy's Lesson

ROBERT had the unfortunate habit of always taking the biggest and best of everything for himself. His brothers, Charlie and Ted, would call him all sorts of names for doing it, but that did not seem to make any difference.

Mother was distressed about it, too, especially as Robert, when invited out to parties, always disgraced the family by his greediness. What could be done? Mother put on her thinking cap, and talked the matter over with her sister, who lived in the next street.

A few days later the boys were delighted to receive an invitation to dinner from their auntie. Remembering all the good things they had enjoyed there in times past, they looked forward to the day of the party with keen anticipation.

At last the day came and dinner time arrived — for which Robert especially had been waiting.

The table was piled with good things, cakes, fruit, jellies, pies, chocolates, and the rest.

Robert's eyes roamed around on the wonderful spread of tasty dishes. "Oh, my!" he thought, "if only I could attend to this little matter all by myself!"

Then he spied a beautiful pear on the fruit dish. It was one of the biggest he had ever seen. There and then he determined to have it sometime during the evening. He also looked around at the other things, and made up his mind which of them he would choose when the plates were passed around.

When all the visitors had been given their places around the table, dinner began. Of course, they all started with bread and butter, in the usual way. Robert, however, soon got tired of that. He wanted that big pie he could see on a plate at the other side of the table. Would he get it in time, or Charlie?

The pies were passed around. Charlie and Ted took small ones, and opened them. "What wonderful centers they have!" thought Robert. "Now, if only I can get that big one."

Robert's turn came. The biggest pie was still there, and of course he took it with joy.

But a disappointment awaited him. As he cut through the top, the whole pie collapsed. It was hollow!

Poor Robert! Tears filled his eyes, but as no one seemed to notice what had happened, he ate the crust as bravely as he could, and said nothing.

The cakes were passed round. Robert felt he was quite justified in taking the biggest this time, seeing there had been nothing in his pie.

But something was wrong with his cake. It looked all right outside, but the center was bitter. What could be the matter? thought Robert. Auntie was generally such a good cook. And then, too, the others didn't seem to be having any trouble at all. It wasn't fair, thought Robert, but he didn't dare say anything for fear the others would laugh at him.

Now came the fruit. How thankful Robert was that the plate was passed down his side of the table first! He felt sure Charlie was after that big pear. Anyhow, he would get it this time.

The plate reached Robert, and he put his hand into the middle of the pile of fruit. Oranges and apples scattered in all directions over the tablecloth, to the consternation of Robert's mother. But Robert got his pear.

His teeth were soon busy, but alas! something seemed to be the matter again. Taking his knife, Robert cut the pear in two. To his utter disgust he found the center was bad.

Still nobody seemed to notice Robert's plight, and no one passed him anything to make up for his misfortunes. Moreover, the others all seemed to be enjoying themselves to the full.

The chocolates came next, and by this time Robert was getting desperate. "I shall have to make up for lost time by taking those two big beauties in the center," he said to himself, as he removed the two best-looking ones from the plate.

"Ugh!" said Robert, groaning inwardly, and blushing all over with disappointment. "What a horrible taste!" Swallowing one with difficulty, he tried the other "to take the taste away," only to find it worse.

On the way home Charlie remarked to Robert about the splendid dinner they had had.

"Splendid what?" said Robert.

"I thought you were not enjoying yourself," said Charlie, "you looked uncomfortable. What was the matter?"

"Matter?" said Robert, "everything I took was bad, even though I did take what looked best every time."

"Maybe that was the cause of the trouble, Robert," said Charlie knowingly. "I think if I were you I would leave the biggest and best-looking things for somebody else next time."

That night Robert stayed awake quite a long time. There were two reasons. One was a pain under his pajama jacket, and the other the advice Charlie had given him. He put "two and two together," and at last decided that the best and safest course for him would be to follow Charlie's suggestion in the future.

© s. w. p.

That night Robert stayed awake quite a long time —!

Safe as a Bank

"Now you won't tell anybody, will you?" said Judy to Gwennie and Ivy. "I've told you because you are my two extra-special friends. It's a great secret, and you mustn't say a word. Promise?"

"We won't say a word," said both together.

"I want you to be safe as a bank," said Judy.

"What does that mean?" asked Ivy.

"That's what my daddy says. Banks have strong rooms which are so protected that thieves can't get anything out of them. I want you to be the same."

Ivy didn't really understand. Anyhow the piece of news that Judy had just communicated was so interesting that she was just itching to tell somebody. She had special friends, too, and it was not long before she met them.

"Now you won't tell anybody, will you?" she said to them, "but I've just heard something awfully interesting that I'm sure you'll be glad to know. Now listen."

Dropping her voice to a whisper, she proceeded to pass on, as well as she could remember, everything that Judy had said.

"But it's a secret," she said, "and Judy says we are not to tell anybody."

"All right," said the others, and went off to find *their* special friends to enlighten them under similar conditions of "secrecy."

Gwennie, however, was different. She thought a good deal of what Judy had said.

"Safe as a bank," she repeated to herself. "That's a good idea. I will try to be like that. And when the thieves come along, I will let them see nothing but the steel bars and padlocks."

It was not long before one came.

"You are one of Judy's special friends, aren't you?" said one of the girls.

"I am," said little Gwennie proudly.

"Do you know if it's true that her uncle has given her $500 and is going to take her for a cruise in the Mediterranean next summer?"

"I'm afraid you will have to ask her yourself," said Gwennie.

"But has she really been given a lot of money?" persisted the questioner.

"If I knew, I couldn't tell you."

"Why not, I'd like to know?" asked the girl.

"Because I'm her bank," you see.

"What, has she given you the money to keep?"

"Oh, no," laughed Gwennie; "but I bank her secrets."

Seeing she could get nothing out of Gwennie, the girl went away. The next day Judy met Gwennie.

"Gwennie," she said, "I feel you are the only true friend I have. My secret is all over the school, and you are the only one who didn't tell."

"How do you know?" asked Gwennie, surprised.

"Because I sent some one to ask you," said Judy, "and she found you as safe as a bank."

Sylvia's Struggle

IF there was one thing more than another that Sylvia disliked, it was practicing on the piano.

She more than disliked it—she hated it.

At the moment, she was in the front room sitting on the piano stool, trying to make her fingers do what the dots on the piece of paper in front of her told them to do.

Tum-tum-tum, thumped Sylvia, Tum-a-tum-tum-tum.

"Oh, dear!" she cried, exasperated. "I can't get the horrid thing right."

Tum-a-tum-a-tum-tum-tum.

"Oh!"

Bang! Sylvia slammed down the lid of the piano.

"I'll never, never practice again," she cried, jumping off the piano stool and running toward the door.

Unfortunately, as she did so, the door opened and in walked mamma.

"Hello, Sylvia, you haven't learned that piece yet, dear, have you?" asked mamma.

"No, and I'm not going to," said Sylvia. "I hate practicing; I hate the old piece; I hate the old piano."

"Sylvia, my dear!" exclaimed mamma. "This won't do. You mustn't give up as easily as that. You'll never get anywhere in life without a struggle. If at first you don't succeed, you must try again."

"I don't want to try again," said Sylvia, pouting.

"Well, let mamma see what she can do with the piece."

So mamma sat down at the piano and tried the piece over. It went so easily, and sounded so very pretty, that Sylvia's frown gradually disappeared.

"It's easy for you," she said, "but I shall never be able to play like that."

"Of course you will, darling," said mamma. "You'll soon be playing this piece better than I can. Anyhow, teacher wants you to play at the school concert at Christmas."

"Me!" exclaimed Sylvia. "Me play at the school concert? Ha! ha! wouldn't they all laugh!"

"I don't see why you shouldn't," said mamma. "There will be other little girls there playing pieces like this, and there's no reason at all why you should let them beat you. All you need is to keep on practicing."

"Practicing!" exclaimed Sylvia. "Practicing! How I hate the very word."

"But you mustn't," said mamma. "It only means learning by doing something over and over again."

"Over and over again," repeated Sylvia. "That's the worst of it. And somehow it never comes the same twice."

"Well, come along and try again now."

Reluctantly Sylvia went back to the piano and started once more while mamma went back to her work.

Tum-tum-tum. Tum-a-tum-tum-tum-tum—

"Oh! It's no good. I can't get it right," she cried, bursting into tears.

She felt she simply couldn't start again, and went over to the sofa to cry it out.

Perhaps she was overtired. I don't know. Anyhow, the very next thing she heard was her name being called from the platform at school. The hall seemed to be full of girls all dressed in their best. Sylvia particularly noticed that they were not in their uniform, and guessed that it must be the Christmas concert.

"Sylvia Silverton," teacher was saying, "will now play for us a delightful little sonata in D minor."

Sylvia started. Was she to play? Evidently. She looked at her dress. Yes, she had on a very beautiful frock which all the girls would admire. It would be very nice, too, going up in front of them all onto the platform. As to the piece, well, she would do her best; and it would be lovely to hear everybody clapping. Perhaps they would want her to come up on the platform again, after she had finished.

And now they *were* clapping. Sylvia flushed, and felt very happy as she walked up the aisle past all her friends, to the platform. Still smiling and blushing, she sat down at the piano and looked at the piece.

Horrors! It was the very piece she had just been practicing. How she wished she had learned it properly. If only she had practiced faithfully. Oh, dear! But there was no turning back now. She simply had to go on, and hope for the best.

Perhaps the girls wouldn't notice the mistakes.

Tum-tum-tum. Tum-a-tum-a-tum-tum-tum-tum-tum.

"He-he-he!" came from the back of the hall.

"Ssh!" whispered the mistress.

Tum-tum-tum.

"He-he-he-he!" laughed somebody out loud.

"Hoo-hoo-hoo-hoo!" chortled another girl, trying hard to keep it in.

It was too much for Sylvia. She slammed down the piano lid and ran from the platform.

Bang!

"Whatever is the matter?" cried mamma, running into the room. "Why, my dear, you've knocked the flowerpot off the window sill. Sylvia!"

"Er-er, where am I?" said Sylvia. "I thought I was at school playing at the concert."

"I wish you had been playing at the piano," said mamma.

"I think I shall practice after this, mamma," said Sylvia, sighing. "It was simply dreadful. I went onto the platform, and found I couldn't play at all. I'll try again, mamma. I really will."

She did; and the concert was a great success after all.

The Strange Fate of Matilda

IT was Dorothy's birthday. The postman had brought a wonderful brown paper parcel, and mother had put it on Dorothy's chair at the breakfast table.

When Dorothy came into the dining room, her eyes opened so wide mother thought they would never shut again. She rushed across the room and started to open the parcel at once. Off came the string and the paper and the lid, and then—

"What a lovely dollie!" she cried. "How good of uncle! He knew just the very thing I wanted. Isn't she a perfect beauty? I believe she even has a wax face. I am going to call her Matilda, and I'm sure I shall love her forever and ever!"

Just then little sister came running into the room.

"What a booful dollie!" she cried. "Do let me hold it just a minute."

"Oh, no, indeed," said Dorothy. "You must never touch Matilda. I will let you look at her sometimes, but mind, you must always leave her alone."

"I want to hold the dollie," cried Jean, stretching out her little arms. "I won't hurt it."

"Get away," said Dorothy angrily. "You must not touch her."

Jean turned away, but there were tears in her eyes. A little later she came back to Dorothy, who was still hugging the dollie, and begged to be allowed to hold it "just for a minute."

"No," said Dorothy. "You may look at her, but you must not touch her. You might break her head, and then what should I do?"

Jean followed Dorothy around all the morning, begging for Matilda. Dorothy went into the garden and put Matilda into her dollie carriage. Still Jean begged.

"I want to hold the dollie," she cried. "I won't hurt it."

"You are not going to hold Matilda,' said Dorothy. "She's mine, and I don't want her broken."

"You are a mean girl," said Jean, tears rolling down her cheeks. "I only want to hold her just a minute."

"Do leave me alone," said Dorothy. "I want to enjoy Matilda all by myself."

But still Jean begged and begged. At last Dorothy rushed indoors and upstairs, Matilda in her arms. Opening a cupboard door, she pushed Matilda inside, intending to keep her out of sight till Jean should have forgotten about her.

Jean was waiting for her at the bottom of the stairs. "Where's that dollie?" she asked. "Do let me hold her just a minute."

"I won't," said Dorothy. "She's gone, anyway."

And so she had, too.

If only Dorothy hadn't been so bad-tempered she would have noticed which cupboard it was that she had put Matilda to sleep in. But being so very angry she had failed to see that it was the cupboard which had the hot-water tank in it. Consequently the longer Matilda lay there the warmer she became. And after a while little tears of wax began to roll down her cheeks. By and by she had no nose left at all and her eyebrows had fallen off.

When at last Dorothy opened the cupboard door again, it was a sorry sight indeed that met her eyes. What she said and what she did had better be left unrecorded. But as she wept and wailed, one thought kept coming to her mind, "If only I had let Jean hold her, this would never have happened!"

And all her life she never forgot this lesson,— that things that are shared often last longer than those one tries to enjoy alone.

Thoughtless Tom

"LOOK at your boots, Tom!" said mamma crossly, "you've been playing football in the mud again. You can't possibly go to school in those boots after dinner. And look at your clothes, mud from head to foot! You *are* a bad boy!"

Tom tried to look sorrowful.

"I'm sorry," he said.

"That's not much good," said his sister Kittie, "it won't get the mud off your clothes."

"And *you* had better not say too much, Kittie," said mamma. "I seem to have spent most of the morning putting things away that you left lying around. I never saw two such thoughtless children in all my life."

"Dinner ready?" asked Tom, changing the subject.

"There you are!" said mamma, "you want your dinner on time, but you never think of all the extra work you give me just because you don't think."

Of course dinner was ready as usual, and Kittie and Tom sat down to theirs while mother tried her best to get the mud off Tom's clothes so that he shouldn't be late for school in the afternoon.

Dinner was soon over, and away went Tom, with a full stomach and an empty head, quite forgetting all his mother had said to him. But he was soon to learn by a lesson he will never forget. It happened the very next day.

*   *   *   *   *

Rip!

Tom was sliding down the branch of a tree in the park when he felt something stick into him. He couldn't stop himself, so there was nothing for it but to leave part of his trousers on the tree. It was an awful gash, and he started to run home as fast as he could go, with one hand holding the pieces together. All the way he was guessing what would happen to him when he arrived. But he was mistaken.

" O Kittie," cried Tom, " look what's happened to my trousers! Where's mamma? "

" Hush! " whispered Kittie. " Mamma's in bed. She was taken ill this morning, and had to send for the doctor. He says she'll be in bed for two or three weeks at least."

" Phew! " whistled Tom; " and what are we going to do? "

" Get on as best we can."

" But how about my trousers? " They must be mended before I can go to school. I'm going upstairs to mamma."

" No, you're not," said Kittie. " The doctor says mamma is not to be disturbed by any one."

" But I *must* get my trousers mended! " fumed Tom.

" Then you must do them yourself."

" You know I can't."

" Well, mamma can't. I suppose I'll have to help you."

All of a sudden Kittie began to realize the extent of the responsibility that had fallen upon her. Together they managed to get some sort of a patch fixed over the gaping hole. Then there was the dinner to get ready — their own dinner. Nothing was ready, nothing cooked, and very little in the cupboard.

" I'll go and buy some things," said Kittie, " if you'll lay the table."

This was a new experience for both of them. Tom was terribly hungry by the time Kittie returned, but there was no use grumbling at her. They ate their meager meal in silence. Then there was the washing up, all the breakfast dishes to do as well, and an excuse to write to the teacher for Kittie, who had to stay at home. What a lot of things there were to do!

" Come back early and help me, won't you, Tom? " pleaded Kittie as Tom ran off to school.

Never had Tom come home so promptly before, even going without his beloved game of football.

" How's mamma? " he asked as he ran in.

" Just the same," said Kittie.

" Well, what do you want me to do? "

" O Tom, I never knew there were so many things to be done. I've been running about ever since you went out of the house, and yet I seem to have done nothing at all. Do get some coal in, and— and — er "

" It's no use crying," said Tom.

" Well, I wish mamma would get better," wept Kittie.

" She will," said Tom hopefully. " Now what about the coal? Give me the scuttle."

As the days passed, Tom began to reveal all the best side of his character. All his thoughtlessness was left behind, because there was no one to help him out of his difficulties except Kittie, and she needed as much help as she gave. Kittie herself learned that she must not expect somebody else to tidy up after her, for if she left anything lying about, *she* was the only one to put it in its place. There was no more grumbling about dinner, because, well, it was their own dinner. If it wasn't cooked just right, they had only themselves to blame.

At last the day arrived when mamma could walk downstairs again. How glad the children were! Not only because mamma was well, but, oh! because there was some one upon whom they could roll the responsibility of everything.

As for mamma, she was so surprised at all she saw and so full of praise for the way the two had managed while she had been away. But most of all she was surprised at Tom.

" What has happened to my thoughtless Tom? " she said, as she saw him chopping the wood, fetching the coal, washing the dishes, and even peeling the potatoes.

" Surely," she said, " this isn't the same boy. The old Tom has disappeared. I shall have to call this one Tom the Thoughtful."

Absolutely Pure

DONALD was a poor little orphan boy who had been taken to one of the big orphan homes just outside of London.

At the time of this story he was in the hospital ward recovering from an attack of mumps or something of the kind. He was just well enough to look at picture books, and took great delight in looking through some big magazines that kind friends had brought.

Being only just able to read, he preferred to look at the advertisements, where most of the words were printed in large, plain letters. Now and then he would call the nurse in charge of the ward to come over to his cot to explain what they meant.

"Nurse," he called on one occasion, "what does this mean?" Slowly he spelled it out: "F-R-Y-S C-O-C-O-A A-B-S-O-L-U-T-E-L-Y P-U-R-E. What does 'absolutely pure' mean?"

"That means," said the nurse kindly, "that it is pure all the way through, that there is nothing bad in it at all, that—er-er, well, that all the bad things have been taken out of it."

"I see," said Donald, evidently satisfied and proceeding to turn over the pages.

Nurse thought he would soon forget all about it. But he didn't.

Nighttime came, and with it Donald's turn to say his prayers. Nurse stood by with bowed head, and listened.

"Dear Jesus," Donald began, "thank you for bringing me here. Thank you for a good bed and nice things to eat. Bless the kind people who look after this hospital. Bless nurse. Bless all the other sick children here and make them better. Bless me and make me a good boy. Bless me and—and—and—and—"

"Go on," whispered the nurse.

"And make me," went on Donald, "make me like Fry's cocoa—"

"Donald!" whispered the nurse, wondering what was coming next.

"Make me like Fry's cocoa," went on Donald, ignoring the gentle admonition, "absolutely pure, so that there is nuffin' bad in me at all. For Jesus' sake, Amen."

What a lovely prayer that was, wasn't it? So innocent and sincere. I am sure the angels pressed near to catch every whispered word.

It's a prayer that you and I should pray, too, isn't it? For that's just what Jesus wants us all to be—"absolutely pure"—or, as the apostle Paul says, "Not having spot, or wrinkle, or any such thing." Eph. 5:27. He wants us to be pure all the way through, with no trace of badness anywhere, and with all the evil things taken away.

Do you want to be like that? I'm sure you do. So pray little Donald's prayer tonight, and Jesus will give you the desire of your heart. Are we not told in His holy word that "if we confess our sins, He is faithful and just to forgive us our sins, and to cleanse us from all unrighteousness"? 1 John 1:9.

What Is Love?

INTO that same orphanage where Donald lived, there came one day a poor little blind boy.

His was a very sad case, for his home had been a dirty, overcrowded back room, and his parents were rough, drunken, and cruel. Indeed, the clean hospital ward, with a comfortable cot all to himself and plenty of nice food to eat, must have seemed like heaven to him.

Johnnie—we'll call him that, for I do not remember his real name—was musical, and one of his dearest wishes was to possess some sort of musical instrument, if only a mouth organ; yet he hardly dared to hope that one would ever be his.

But some days later, Christmas came, and with it a number of brown paper parcels from kind friends for the children in the ward. Oh, joy! There was one for Johnnie, too.

Nurse cut the string and guided the little hands as they unfolded the paper. Johnnie's face suddenly lit up with a delighted smile. "It *is* a mouth organ," he said. "Who could have sent it to me?"

"There's a piece of paper here," said the nurse. "Shall I read you what it says? It's from a little girl who likes to send things to children in this hospital."

"Yes, do," said Johnnie.

"It doesn't say very much," said the nurse, "just, 'With lots of love.' "

" 'Lots of love,' " repeated Johnnie slowly. "What's that?"

"Don't you know what love is?" asked the nurse, her eyes suddenly filling with tears.

"No," said Johnnie, "I've never heard of that. What is it?"

Nurse was silent for a moment. What could she say? How could she explain what love was? She had never met anybody before, not even the youngest child, who did not understand love.

"Don't *you* know what it means, nurse?" asked Johnnie, wondering at her silence.

"Oh, poor little Johnnie!" cried the nurse, suddenly flinging her arms around the little chap and kissing him, "That is love, dear. I can't explain it any better."

She held him tightly for a few moments, and kissed him again. It was Johnnie who broke the silence.

"I like love," he whispered; "it feels so nice."

More tears ran down the nurse's face as she looked at the little blind face, smiling so sweetly now because some one had loved him at last.

As I heard this sad story, I wondered how many others there are, poor little unloved boys and girls —and maybe older people, too—who are waiting for some one to speak a kindly word to them, to do a gentle deed, to show them what love is. Perhaps there are some love-starved hearts near you. Won't you look around at school and see? And maybe at home, as well? For I'm fairly certain that both father and mother would be glad, too, for a little more love than they get.

The House That Glowed

IT was Christmas Eve, and poor little Johann, driven out of his home by an angry and brutal stepfather, was trudging wearily through the snow.

His coat was ragged, and sodden with melted snow. His shoes were worn and split at the seams, so that his feet were numb with cold. His quaint cap, pulled well down over his ears and forehead, had a gaping tear that let in the biting wind.

Night was falling, and the gathering darkness found the homeless little boy still plodding on his sad and lonely way.

"If only I could find some shelter, some place where I could get warm, and the wind would not chill me so," he thought to himself. "If only some one would give me some food to eat, and something hot to drink!"

Coming to the edge of the forest, he caught sight of a little village nestling in the valley below, with several fine, large houses dotting the hillside all around. Lights were already twinkling in the windows, while the smoke from many chimneys, curling upward, blended with the murky sky.

A great new hope sprang up in little Johann's heart. Here at last, among so many lovely homes, he would find some one to care for him. He walked more quickly, so sure he was that his troubles were almost over.

Soon he came to the entrance of a fine, big mansion. There were many lights in the windows and a very bright one over the front door. Surely, he thought, people who could live in such a house must have lots of money and would be only too pleased to help a poor, hungry little boy.

Very bravely he walked up to the front door, and, by standing on tiptoe, managed to catch hold of the handle of the bell. He pulled it hard, and there was such a noise inside that it frightened him. But he was more frightened still when the great oak door was thrown back and a big man dressed in the finest clothes looked out at him.

"Did you ring that bell?" asked the haughty butler, frowning.

"Y-y-y-yes," stammered Johann, "I-I-I'm very cold and hungry, and I thought you—"

"This is Christmas Eve," snapped the butler, "and the house is full of guests. I'm sorry, but we haven't time to bother with the likes of you just now. Good night."

And the door was shut.

"Oh!" said Johann to himself, "I never thought any one would do that. But perhaps they are too busy here. I must try somewhere else."

So he walked on down into the village itself, passing by the other big mansions for fear the people inside might also be too busy to care about hungry little boys on Christmas Eve.

From the first house he reached there came sounds of music and laughter, and feeling sure that there must be very friendly people living there, he knocked gently on the door. But there was so much noise inside that he had to knock again and again, each time louder than before.

At last the door swung open, and a young man wearing a funny paper cap looked out.

"Excuse me," said Johann, "but I wondered if you could—"

"Sorry," cried the gay young man, "we're having a Christmas Eve party in here, and we can't stop now."

"But please, please!" pleaded Johann.

"Sorry; good night!" cried the young man. And bang! the door was shut.

Terribly disappointed, Johann went next door, but the people there were making so much noise that they didn't even hear him at all, loud as he knocked.

At the next house a crabby old gentleman merely told him to run home and not bother the neighbors. Run home, indeed!

At another house he was told to call again another day. They would help him then, perhaps, the people said. But he needed help now!

So, going from house to house through the entire village, he sought shelter and food, and found none.

Almost hopeless and heartbroken he trudged out into the night, leaving the twinkling lights behind him. He felt he could lie down and die in the road, he was so tired, so hungry, so discouraged.

Just then he happened to look up and found himself passing a tiny, tumbledown old cottage, so dark and dismal that he probably wouldn't have seen it at all but for the white carpet of snow on the ground showing it up. A blind covered the one window, but faint streaks of light gleamed from under the door and through cracks in the woodwork.

Johann stood still and wondered what he should do.

Should he knock here?

What would be the use? Surely if the people who lived in all the big houses—who had money for lovely parties and things—couldn't afford to help a poor boy, how could the folk in a house like this? No, it was of no use. Better not bother them. Better go on and die in the woods.

Then he thought again. He had knocked at so many houses, there could be no harm in trying one more. So he turned from the road up the snow-covered garden path and tapped gently on the door.

A moment later the door opened cautiously, and an elderly woman peered out. "Bless my soul!" she exclaimed. "Whatever are you doing out there in the cold tonight?"

"Please—" began Johann.

But before he could say another word she had flung the door wide open and dragged him inside.

"You poor little child," she exclaimed. "Deary, deary me! You look so cold and hungry. Half starved, or I'm mistaken. And wet through. Let's get those things off at once. Wait a moment while I stir up the fire and put the kettle on."

Johann looked about him and saw that the little one-roomed cottage was as bare as could be, without even a carpet on the floor. The light he had seen through the crack came from one lone candle set on the mantelpiece. But he hadn't time to see much else, for the kind woman was soon stripping off his wet rags, wrapping him in a blanket, and setting him up at the table before a bowl of steaming soup.

Then she went back to stir the pot on the stove. As she did so she suddenly noticed something and looked up.

Was it a dream, or were her eyes deceiving her? The candlelight had given place to a warm and lovely glow that seemed to be getting brighter every minute, filling every corner of the cottage with a heavenly radiance. Every drab piece of furniture seemed to be shining and glistening like burnished gold as when God filled the temple with His glory.

And the rich man, looking down from his mansion on the hill, suddenly exclaimed, "There's a strange light in the valley. Look! Widow Greatheart's cottage is on fire!"

The news spread swiftly from house to house, and soon all the gay parties were abandoned as the people, wrapping themselves up in their coats and shawls, rushed out to see what was the matter.

They saw the light, too, and running toward the widow's cottage, beheld the poor tumbledown old building glowing like an alabaster bowl.

Peering inside, all they could see was the dear old woman caring for the very same little boy who had called that night at all their homes.

Then, as the light faded, they knocked on the door to ask anxiously what could have happened.

"I really do not know," said Widow Greatheart, with a smile of wondrous joy and satisfaction on her face. "I just seemed to hear a voice saying to me, 'Inasmuch as ye have done it unto one of the least of these My children, ye have done it unto Me.' "